Conrad

SHARON BEZA

InfusedMedia Co. LLC
www.infusedmedia.co
1-888-251-6088

For my son Drew, whose lifelong dream
is for all animals to be protected

I wish to thank my family and friends for love and support. My children Michael,Drew and Nathan who inspire me. My grandkids Samantha and Lucas. I love all of you. Dad and John you've never left us. All my babies Barbie, Cruiser we hold you. And to my artist Madeline Savarese, You're the best. And to the people who take the time to buy and read my books, Thank you from the bottom of my heart. Love Sharon

Darlene was a big girl now, almost eleven years old. She wanted to be treated as such, so she would let her mom know this very day that she wanted to go into the garden unaccompanied to plant her flowers and just feel the sun on her face. After all, this was a vacation, and she intended to enjoy herself. And it was safe in the garden. Her father had made sure of that.

The cabin in the forest was well made. Her father, an architect, had built a safe habitat for his little girl. It was simply paradise. Darlene knew every nook and cranny in the fenced enclosure, having spent many of her young years there, and she absolutely loved it.

Darlene's mom looked over at her young daughter and saw how Darlene meticulously arranged all the plants and flowers she wanted to plant in the garden. Her daughter's lips were pursed into a straight line, and she looked very determined about her work. Darlene had been blind since birth, so her parents kept a special watch over her, but lately they had to admit the bright and carefree Darlene was starting to try to spread her wings a little bit.

And so at that moment, Darlene decided to confront her mother. She called out, "Mom, I believe it's time to allow me some alone time to try to do things on my own. I want to start by planting these flowers in the garden by myself and to show you what I can do. Then you can come outside and check it out." She giggled. "I want to impress you with my gardening skills."

"I don't know, Darlene," her mother started. "If you got hurt …"

"Mom!" Darlene objected. "Kids do get hurt sometimes. It's part of growing up, and I know my way around this whole place. Please. I'm blind but not helpless."

"Oh, Darlene." Her mom walked up and put her arms around her daughter. "This I do know. I'll tell you what. Today is the day you'll plant the flowers on your own. Of course you must keep your phone around your neck at all times, just in case. Please; that would make me feel better."

"Yes!" Darlene squealed. "I can do that!"

Her mother smiled as Darlene carefully carried the box and opened the back door. Using her cane, she cautiously started for the garden. Walking a little ways behind her daughter, she then closed the door.

She wanted to rush out and accompany Darlene, but she stopped herself. It was time for the young girl to try something on her own. So she just watched as Darlene slowly disappeared down the path.

Oh, this is fantastic! I feel free, to say the least, Darlene thought. She knew every step down the path, and it didn't take long to reach the garden. She set the box down and slowly felt along the edge of the flower bed her dad had built for her. Maybe she couldn't see her flowers, but she could inhale them and arrange them in a vase for everyone to enjoy.

She now busied herself for a while until she heard a small whimpering sound. Then the whimpering got louder.

Darlene got down on her knees and crawled to the fence. She put her hand out toward the sound of the crying. It made her think of a baby. As her fingers went through the holes, she felt something trying to lick them. The tongue was very rough.

"Oh, a kitten!" she exclaimed. "A poor kitten." She then cooed to it. "Are you hungry? You sure sound hungry."

She remembered the snacks her mom had put in her backpack. She pulled out the chicken sandwich and broke off small pieces to stick through the fence. The kitten ate hungrily. She then put milk in her thermos lid and pushed it under the fence.

She talked to the kitten. "Where's your mama? Are you lost?"

She heard a strange purring sound and then the rustling of the leaves as the animal left the area. She called out to it, "You'll be okay. Come back tomorrow."

But who would be coming back tomorrow? She thought. She decided she would call the kitten Conrad after a handsome young man in one of her mom's books.

"Bye, Conrad. See you soon," she whispered.

At that moment, the phone rang. It was her mom, and she wanted to know if it were time to be impressed.

"Yes, Mother." Darlene giggled. "It sure is."

The next day Darlene packed her own lunch.

Her mom watched her. "My, oh my, sweetie, you sure have a big appetite today."

"Yes, Mother," Darlene replied. "It is because I may stay a little longer outside today. I'm having so much fun, and I love it in the garden. So see you later, okay?"

Her mom gave the usual speech. "Be careful. Don't take any chances."

"Yes, Mother." Darlene made for the door.

"I'll check on you later, dear," her mom called out as the young girl carefully headed down the path.

Soon in the garden, Darlene felt the edge of the flower box and sat down beside it. She put her stuff alongside and reached for her watering can. Within minutes, she heard the crackling of the leaves and then the strange purring.

"Conrad? Is that you?" she called softly.

She once again put small pieces of meat through the holes in the fence. The kitten ate hungrily and licked at her fingers.

This went on for several weeks as the family's vacation continued. Then Darlene decided to do something she knew she wasn't supposed to do. She wanted to pet Conrad and maybe hold him. Was that so wrong? He was her friend now, and she knew she'd be very careful. She wouldn't even go outside the gate. Conrad could come inside.

So the next day when the leaves started to rustle, she was ready. Feeling her way to the gate, she reached up and unlocked it. It flew open, and a fast fur ball ran past.

Soon she felt a wet nose sniffing her face and said aloud, "Conrad, I opened up the gate so we could actually meet, cat to girl." She laughed softly and then reached out to touch his fur.

The cat drew back, but then she felt his head begin to nudge against her body. "Well, Conrad, nice to meet you too," she whispered. Then she remembered. "Oh! You must be hungry."

She tried to feed him, but he bit at the food quickly and

then tried to take the whole piece of chicken out of her hand. "No, Conrad," she softly reprimanded him, but she realized he probably was just hungry.

As he was eating, Darlene reached out and gently petted his body. "Wow!" she gasped. "You're sure getting big eating all this food."

After every morsel of it was gone, the cat purred that strange purr. She felt him sniffing at her again, and then the phone rang. Faster than lightning, Conrad was gone. Darlene's mom was calling. As quickly as she could, the young girl located the gate and latched it closed.

After a couple more weeks of feeding and getting to know Conrad, it all just stopped. On that last day, he simply didn't show up at the garden.

Darlene was heartbroken. She called out, "Conrad! Conrad!"

But there was no rustling of the leaves, no strange purring sound, and no more nudging of his head against her body.

Her mother noticed Darlene's sad demeanor. "My goodness, sweetie, you look like you've just lost your best friend."

I have, Darlene thought. He was her secret, and now he was gone. She didn't mind heading back to the city. Without Conrad, it just wasn't the same. As they drove down the mountain, she whispered out the window, "Stay safe, my friend. I'll miss you."

As the years passed, Darlene still visited the cabin every year. She waited in the garden, hoping for a sign of her friend. She grew into a smart and beautiful young lady. In the city, she excelled at her school. She hoped to follow in her mom's footsteps and become an author. Then she could live in the cabin in the forest.

As her sixteenth birthday approached, her parents asked her, "Where do you want to go for your special dinner?"

"The cabin," she answered.

Her father raised his eyebrows. "The cabin?" he repeated.

"Yes, Daddy. I love it there. Please! I want to have my birthday there. We could do barbeque."

"Well, Darlene, I did ask you." He smiled. "Weather permitting, barbeque it is! I'll drop you and your mother off early, and then I have a few things in the city to finish up. I'll join you two on the weekend. That way, everything will be ready. Sound like a plan?"

"Oh, yes, Daddy! Thank you!" Darlene reached out and gave her father a big hug.

***

In the middle of the city, the chief of police entered the briefing room and informed his officers, "An extremely dangerous convict named Sullivan has escaped from an area hospital. He has managed to steal a vehicle from the parking lot. I have a description of him and the car. It is top priority to recapture this man."

***

Unaware of any danger, Darlene's parents did something they swore they'd never do, but their independent daughter could be very persuasive. She had managed to talk them into dropping just her off early at the cabin so she could relax and get some of her own writing done. In her sanctuary, she could think more clearly. Besides, her mom and dad both had last-minute birthday surprises to attend to. Darlene had her life alert around her neck at all times so they felt pretty comfortable she'd be okay.

***

The chief knew if Sullivan made it out of the city, they'd be in trouble. The forest would have too many places to hide, and the people in the cabins would be vulnerable. It was time to warn the media. The police needed all the help they could get to find this killer.

***

While shopping, Darlene's mother called to check on her daughter.

"All is well, Mother."

"Good then. I'll continue on." Her mom laughed. "I'll see you soon."

"Okay, Mom."

And as she hung up the phone, Darlene noticed a change in the temperature outside. She sat down on the bench and checked the weather report. Sure enough, there was cooler temperature and rain in the forecast. She would go into the house soon, and her parents would arrive in the morning.

***

Driving the speed limit, the escapee knew his way around the area and was already an hour on the freeway. He drove on until he neared the cutoff to the forest. He needed gas, but he knew he couldn't take the chance to stop. He drove slowly through the small town. He knew there would be empty cabins higher up, so that was where he made his way.

As he drove up the road, he passed a small convenience store and continued driving past. A man pumping gas saw him and waved. The killer waved back.

After he finished pumping his gas, the man went into the store to buy some coffee. As he started to pay, he stared up at the breaking news on the TV. "You're not going to believe this, but I'm pretty sure that same guy drove past here."

"You're kidding!" the clerk replied as he frantically called 9-1-1.

***

The sheriff then let the LAPD know the killer had been spotted in the small town. Now Chief O'Hara would have to hurry. They'd need a tracker, so he called his good friend, Darrell, to get his dog and meet him as soon as possible.

***

In a local eatery, Darlene's parents saw the bulletin as well and panicked. First, they called Darlene to warn her. They told her to get inside and lock all of her doors. She then pushed her life alert.

"You'll be okay, sweetie," her dad told her. "We're coming!"

At the meeting place, Chief O'Hara waited for backup and the tracker. Inside the cabin, Darlene was locking up everything the best she could. She tried not to worry. The convict was seen down the mountain on the road. He could possibly drive right out of the area. Darlene's mom and dad were leaving the city to come be with her. Everything would be fine. She was sure of it.

But it wasn't. The killer felt the car's engine sputter as the gas ran out. He'd managed to turn off the main road and guide the car into the trees off to the side of the road. He got out and looked around. It was starting to get dark outside. He felt the chill in the air as he started trekking through the trees. In the distance, he saw lights and headed in that direction. He needed warm clothes and food.

Darlene moved carefully through the cabin, checking everything she could. She was being watched as she did so. The eyes moved silently toward the cabin. All of a sudden, Darlene heard a knock at the door. The convict held a thick branch in his hand. Inside, Darlene crouched in a corner, terror filling her entire body. *Maybe it's the chief. Mom and Dad had contacted them for me.*

She called out softly, "Yes?"

On the other side of the door, she heard an answer. "I need help. My car is out of gas down the road. Can I borrow some?"

Now Darlene knew it wasn't the chief. "No, I'm sorry. We have no gas here."

"Can I come inside to warm myself? It's quite cold out here," the convict asked.

"No, I'm sorry, but you can't come in. I'm sick." Darlene was getting shaky now.

The convict knew one thing at this moment: this girl was all alone. He then took the branch and struck the window.

Darlene moved quickly now. She made her way to the back door. She stopped and quickly listened. She heard the glass breaking and the sound of someone starting to enter the house. She carefully opened the back door and slipped out. It was raining as she made her way down the path. She headed to the garden, and kneeling in the cold, she waited.

"Where is this girl?" Sullivan angrily hissed.

He searched the home quickly and found nothing. He grabbed a few items and then opened the back door. He looked out and thought he saw something moving. He then turned on the flashlight and started down the path.

Darlene heard the door open and then noise coming toward her. *I will be found.* She had to get to the forest. She crawled quickly along until she felt the gate. She stood halfway up, unlatched it, and let herself out. She thought she could hide better in the trees.

She started carefully toward them, and then the unthinkable happened. In her panic, her foot went down in a hole, and feeling a snap, she cried out in pain before she could stop herself.

In the distance, she heard a laugh. The killer then called out to the frightened Darlene, "You shouldn't have been so unfriendly, girl."

She could now hear him coming toward her, and she whimpered softly, knowing she had nowhere else to go. Suddenly, she felt a rush of air go by her quickly and heard a bloodcurdling scream and thrashing sounds that didn't last long.

She waited, shaking in the cold. Soon she felt a presence and then heard a familiar purring sound. She carefully reached out her hand. She remembered the feel of that fur, but the cat was bigger now, much bigger.

As the giant animal curled his body around the girl, she whispered, "My sweet kitten, you're here again. I missed you so much!" She once again felt that familiar nudge against her face.

***

Officer Darrell had been with the police force for more than sixteen years. He was an expert tracker, so when he received the chief's call, he hurried to the meeting place with his dog. Darlene's parents' frantic call told them their daughter was blind and alone in the cabin.

After the young girl pushed her alert button, the officer knew there had to be trouble. They made their way to the address. The cabin was located higher in the mountain, and Darrell started up on foot with the dog that picked up a scent right away.

"He's got him!" Darrell yelled out.

As they neared the cabin, the dog ran straight for the porch. They could see the smashed window. They now entered the house with guns drawn. The dog ran ahead, sniffing the ground. The chief made a sign to Darrell to follow the dog. The chief and another officer had the house.

The tracker cautiously followed behind as the dog made his way to the back door. Darrell reached out and opened it. A small light shone in the distance. Very agitated now, the dog broke into a run.

"Give it up, Sullivan!" Darrell called out loudly. "This is the police!"

Gun drawn and ready, he followed the dog. Darlene heard the tracker call out and the sound of the barking animal. Conrad then rose up.

She could feel his fur stiffen. "I know you must go," she whispered to him. "Thank you for saving me. I love you so much." She felt the familiar nudge, and then he was gone.

As Darrell continued on, he prepared to confront the convict. But as he reached the barking dog, he saw a body. It was Sullivan, and it was clear that he was dead with his throat ripped out. Darrell looked around quickly and saw nothing.

But as he shined the light around the body, he saw the giant footprints. He'd seen prints like those more than five years ago in a cabin further up. The ATF had raided it, and several exotic animals had been seized. *Could it be?* thought Darrell.

All at once, Darlene's feeble voice called out, "Help me, please! I'm over here!"

Darrell ran to her as the dog excitedly barked a warning.

The chief's call came over the radio. "Darrell, come in."

Darrell spoke back immediately. "It's over, Chief. Sullivan is dead. It looks like a mountain lion beat us to him. I have the girl. She's hurt but alive."

"We will be right there," came the reply.

Darrell then bent down and comforted Darlene. As he put his coat over her, he asked the young girl, "Do you know what happened? Did you hear anything?"

She lifted her face and simply said, "It was Conrad, and he came back for me."

Darrell knew two things at that moment: the convict was stopped, and the girl was protected. He then said, "Yes,

Darlene, he did come back." And with that thought, he began to brush away the giant prints.

Not the End

Ti-ger (noun): a very large, solitary cat with a yellow-brown coat striped with black

***

Darlene sat in the garden a few days after the killing and waited. Things had quieted down after the police and detectives were done with their investigation. She had been in the garden every day, hoping and praying he would come, and on the fourth day, he did. With the gate open, she sat alone on the bench.

Feeling his presence, she softly called out to him, "Conrad, my sweet, sweet kitten."

As the cat strode up to her, she reached out and touched his head and marveled at the mere size of it. "Oh my," she whispered out loud, "you've really grown." She continued talking to him as she scratched his ears. The strange purring started softly and then grew louder as the girl giggled at the big head.

"I know now what you are, Conrad. I don't know how you found me, but I thank God you did. I thought of you every day and prayed for your safety. Did you think of me? I'm so glad you came back. I've missed you so. How did you know? Where were you all this time? I can't lose you again, my sweet kitten. Promise you'll stay close to me. I love you so much." With tears streaming down her face, Darlene kissed the massive head.

***

After asking Darlene if she knew Conrad was a tiger, Darrell had left the girl as lots of thoughts swirled in his head. As he drove to the dinner party, he had a big smile on his face. Now that his good friend John O'Hara was chief of police, they would have more time to spend together, and he would enjoy that. Maybe they could even get some fishing time in.

With Darrell and his army buddy being so close, he knew they should know about the secret on the mountain. He was sure—actually had a gut feeling—this creature wouldn't be a problem. After all, it seemed it was quite the opposite.

As he entered the room, he saw O'Hara and called out to him. "Congratulations! Now we'll be in touch more, and we need to talk."

"Is everything okay?" the chief asked Darrell.

"Yes, but I believe I'll need yours as well. But for now, let's celebrate, Chief."

"I'll drink to that." O'Hara laughed.

And they did.

M. Savarese '19

The Beginning

He had hidden here many times before, so when the loud noises and smoke came, he cowered in his hiding place and shook. The odor of the strangers wafted through the air. He heard his mother cry out in pain as something struck her mighty body.

He wanted to come out from his hiding spot, but fear kept him glued there. When it had quieted down, his thirst overcame him, and he slowly crawled out from the hole. He whimpered for his mother, but she was no longer in the enclosure. He found chaos in the yard. Everyone and everything was gone, and it was eerily still.

The giant metal door was wide open. He drank some water quickly and then cautiously made his way to the opening. Since there was no one there to stop him, he slowly walked through.

He began to look for his mother, but she was nowhere to be found. *Maybe she's out in the forest*, he wondered. So he headed to the trees. His small feet felt funny underneath him. Wobbling over several logs, he lost his footing and rolled quickly down a small embankment.

As he came safely to a stop, he realized this new world

was very different from the enclosure. It was scary but exciting too. He continued on a while before he felt tired and weary. Stopping by a large tree, he saw an indent. He nestled down inside and soon fell fast asleep.

As he awoke, he felt a rumble in his tummy. He was hungry, and he cried out loud. He waited, but no one came for him. Not his mother or the man who brought the food. He continued forward when all at once a bird flew down at him and tried to peck his ears. He made a loud noise that scared it away, and then he ran fast to get far from the pesky thing.

He walked a long distance before stepping into a puddle of water and then lapped up most of it. An odor gently circled through the air, so he continued toward it. Soon noises followed, so he decided to investigate.

From afar, he saw a human figure bent over inside a fence. She was small and didn't look very scary, like the big men he was used to, so he took a couple of steps to get a closer look.

There was something very different about this human. He sniffed the air and smelled food. Before he could stop himself, he whimpered loudly.

The startled girl then spoke. "Hello there." He hesitated, and then a sweet voice called out again, "Where are you? Are you lost?"

He watched as the human put her small fingers through the hole in the fence. He couldn't contain himself and quickly made his way toward her. Softly, he licked her fingers.

"Oh, a kitten!" She spoke loudly. "Are you hungry? You sure sound hungry."

She proceeded to feed him small pieces of chicken through the holes and then pushed a small cup of sweet milk under the fence. He lapped it up quickly and finished the meat just as fast. He smelled the girl's scent again and felt comfortable.

After a while, he tired and soon left to find a place to sleep. After walking a while, he found a small hole and lay down. He slept fitfully, dreaming of his mother. He awoke several times. Alone and scared, he burrowed deeper and deeper. When daylight came once more, he ventured out until he found another small puddle left from the rain and drank his fill.

He walked and walked but never found his mother. Suddenly, he heard a sweet voice calling out, "Conrad, Conrad!" His curiosity aroused once more, he started toward the sound.

When he was in sight of the garden, he saw the girl bent down, calling out that name, Conrad. As he got closer, he whimpered softly and then jumped as she screamed out excitedly that he was there.

"Oh, my sweet, sweet kitten," she cooed to him.

Then like before, she fed him lots of good food and sweet milk. He then purred at her, a weird sound he'd never made before. He liked this human and decided he would find a place to sleep closer to her. He nestled down in some leaves by a tree. Safe and warm, he slumbered a peaceful sleep with sweet dreams this time.

Darlene

Days went by as Conrad continued to visit the girl. On one particular day, she actually opened the gate, and he ran in fast, old habits being hard to break. As he stood near this human, she reached out and touched him. Since it was his first time to be petted, he reacted quickly, but sensing no danger, he allowed it and actually kind of enjoyed it. Only his mother had ever lovingly touched him.

All of a sudden, he jolted and ran out as a noise emitted from the girl. He watched from a distance as she relocked the gate. A protective feeling stirred in his body. He kept his eye on her as she walked the path from the garden to the big house at the end. She stepped slow and steady, and he realized there was a difference about her. He made sure she reached the steps before he left to go nap.

Turning, he saw another human waiting for her and heard laughter and a voice call out, "Hurry, Darlene! Come in quickly. It's starting to rain."

As the time went by, Conrad grew fast. The birds no longer flew at him, seeing how he managed to grab one quickly in his mouth. He downed it quickly and realized he seemed hungrier and hungrier, even with Darlene's feedings.

One cloudy day, something happened that would change everything. He woke up early as a light rain was falling. Something just didn't feel right in the air, so he crept cautiously about in his regular territory. He was just about to enter a clearing when a loud boom sounded. He immediately froze. Transfixed to the spot ahead, he watched as several men walked toward an injured deer.

One lifted his arm, and the booming sound again rang out. In horror, he heard laughter as the screaming of the poor animal ended suddenly. In shock and fear, he cowered from these men. He knew she'd be waiting, but danger was in the air. He circled around them and headed as far away as he could. He thought he heard her calling him, "Conrad, Conrad."

He knew now that remote place beyond was beckoning him. He would be safe there. He would try to come back for her when he felt the time was right and watch the garden, listening for that sweet, sweet voice.

Epilogue

With sadness on her face, Darlene entered the cabin. "Mom," she said softly, "the hunters were close again."

"Yes, sweetie, I heard. I'll talk to your father. Are you okay, dear? You look like you just lost your best friend."

I have, Darlene thought. *I have*. Her fear turned to anguish as she fought back the horrible thoughts. She knew the hunters were close. She heard the awful sounds of their guns. Conrad was safe. She was sure of it. Even so, her mind would not be stilled. She felt an intense feeling of fear. She waited and waited, longing for her friend until at long last the family had to leave the cabin and head back to the city.

Tiger Lily

The mother and father sat on the bench, wrapped in each other's arms. The man held his distraught wife close as she cried.

"I only took my eyes off her a minute," she said between sobs. "I looked everywhere, but I just couldn't find her. Oh, my poor baby, Mommy's so sorry."

The father tried to comfort her, but deep down inside, he was afraid. The campgrounds were relatively safe, but further into the forest, it could become dangerous.

As they waited for the authorities, the child's siblings searched for the four-year-old, calling out her name, but they got no answer. The older brother asked his dad if he could search closer to the trees, but the concerned father was fearful of him getting lost as well. With tears in his eyes, he hugged the boy close. As the authorities arrived, they collected information from the family.

Mrs. Sisson had been packing up the camp. All the children were inside the tent playing.

"I saw Claire in there with the others, so I continued on with my packing and picking up outside. If something happens to her, it will be all my fault," she blurted out.

"Okay, ma'am," Chief O'Hara said. "If you can remember, we need to get a timeline of how long you think your daughter has been missing."

"Oh, she's been gone … I'm sorry to say …" The upset mom went on. "Maybe a half hour, maybe more." And with that, she ran to the bench and cried again.

Mr. Sisson seemed calmer, so they asked him a couple of questions.

"Was there anyone you noticed near your camp this morning?"

"I didn't see anyone," he replied, "but then I had taken the dog out, and we had walked away. I never saw or heard Claire. Is there a reason you're asking?"

"It's just procedure," the chief replied.

"Well, all I do know is that my daughter is out there somewhere and we need to find her soon."

"I realize that, Mr. Sisson. We've got the search party here now. They're gearing up to head out. We'll find your daughter." He patted the child's father on the shoulder.

***

Toddling along, Claire saw the pretty lilies; she liked to pick flowers with her sister Molly. She looked around but didn't see Molly, but she spied more flowers and headed in that direction.

After playing awhile, she tried to find her mom. She looked around and walked and walked, but all she saw were trees. She called out for her mother, but her mom didn't answer. So she walked some more. She got thirsty and took a drink from the sippy cup she carried, but more than that, she was getting tired.

***

The search party was looking for the child within minutes of being informed of the situation. Broken off in groups, they had entered the forest.

In a cabin up on the mountain, a young woman listened to her radio while she finished some light housework. Her phone rang, and she immediately knew who it would be.

"Darlene, did you hear?" the voice on the other line asked. "A child is missing from the campgrounds."

"Yes, Mother, I did. I'm praying they find her quickly and safely. It's colder at night, we know, and the sun will be going down in a while."

"Yes," Darlene's mom agreed. "Well, Dad and I will see you soon, dear. Is there anything you'd like us to pick up before we leave?"

"Yes," Darlene answered. "Ice cream. I know it's cold outside, but I still would like to have some on hand."

"Well, okay, sweetheart. You'll get it. See you soon, dear." She hung up the phone.

Darlene stood out on the porch. Her sightless eyes stared ahead, but even still, she could tell snow would come soon.

The search party continued looking and calling out to the lost child, but each group came up empty-handed. The police had set up a base camp, and as the searchers regrouped and rested, each noticed the distraught parents with the siblings clinging to each other in their hope of finding Claire.

"Have you heard from Darrell yet?" the chief asked one of the officers.

"Yes, he's on his way with his dog now. It will be awhile, though. He's a bit away," the officer replied.

"Well," continued O'Hara, "we'll keep searching until dark. After that, it's dangerous."

As the sun started to go down, everyone realized it was looking dim. With no water or food, the child would weaken, and she only had on a light jacket.

***

Claire was tired. She wanted her mama and daddy. She wanted to go home and crawl into her bed. She held her sippy cup tightly and softly cried. As it started to get colder and darker, she sat down by a big tree. She heard strange noises and was scared. She again sipped out of the small cup with the unicorn on it. Then she held it against her chest for comfort. She started to get sleepier and sleepier. Her eyes were half-closed when she saw him. Gigantic, he slowly moved toward her.

She reached out, gently touching his face. "Big kitty," she said as she closed her eyes.

***

Darrell drove fast toward the camp. It was starting to get dark. The search teams were starting to return. He looked at his dog. "You ready, boy?" he called out to him.

Rusty immediately responded with a loud bark.

"Me too." Darrell laughed. "Me too."

***

Darlene readied herself for bed and knelt down to pray. She prayed for several things: her parents, the missing child, and her best friend. "Please, Father in heaven, keep them all safe. In Jesus's name. Amen."

Happy her parents were driving up the next day, the sleepy young woman climbed into her warm bed. Nighttime came, and so did the snow, very light, but with it came the cold. Although a helicopter flew over the trees with night vision, they could pick not up anything.

***

Darrell arrived, and several people ran over to greet him. He quickly got all the stats and prepared himself and Rusty for departure.

"How're the parents holding up?" he asked the chief.

"Well, the father is still here, but the mother and siblings left a while ago with relatives. A storm is coming. What do you think?"

"I need to leave now," Darrell answered.

"Yeah, I know," the chief went on, "but keep me posted."

"Will do then."

With Rusty leading the way, the two headed into the forest. The dog sniffed around but didn't pick up the little girl's scent. He could track on sight, so both continued to walk forward.

Light snow was falling, and Darrell knew that wasn't good. They kept going, and then Rusty growled low in his throat. He looked at Darrell for the nod, and when he got it, he started to run.

"Find her, boy," encouraged the tracker.

***

As Darlene awoke, she immediately smelled snow. She carefully made her way to the back door, and as she opened it up, the cold air rushed in, and tiny snowflakes hit her face.

"Oh!" she gasped and quickly closed the door.

She put on some coffee and thought of her parents. They should arrive soon—and she hoped—safely. Her thoughts turned to the missing child. *Had they found her?* she wondered.

She turned on the news, and of course the talk was all about the missing child.

"Oh, no!" Darlene said under her breath. "They haven't found her yet."

She stared straight ahead, eyes unseeing, and her memories came flooding through her mind.

"Conrad, my sweet, sweet kitten," she spoke softly aloud.

***

Darrell followed Rusty as he ran ahead sniffing and growling. Soon it was a full-blown howl, yet the dog had stopped and was sniffing the ground frantically. He then abruptly turned around.

"What is it, boy?" Darrell called out.

As they walked in the direction past the stream, Rusty again turned in a circle. The tracker shined the flashlight down and saw the tracks of a mountain lion. The tracks had gone forward when they did an about-face and then entered the water. The dog waited for the signal to cross.

"No, boy. I'm not feeling this." Darrell signaled for him to go forward.

They continued onward for quite a while with Rusty

continuing to sniff the ground. As he turned a bend, he stopped dead in his tracks and howled a sound only Darrell understood. He walked toward his trusted companion. The light again shone down on footprints, giant ones they both had seen before.

"Oh, boy!" Darrell let out. "Oh, boy!"

He collared the excited dog, and then together they cautiously moved in a straight line. Up ahead by a tree, the giant beast's eyes shone into Darrell's. With a low growl in its throat, the mighty cat rose up off the ground. The tracker could see a small child lying beside the tree.

"It's okay, Conrad." Darrell spoke aloud. "We're here to take over."

The little girl sat up slowly. Unafraid of her newfound friend, she pulled on his neck to lift herself up. Conrad sniffed her gently.

"My goodness, Claire," Darrell said to the little girl. "We have been worried about you, but I see you've been in good hands, so to speak."

"Big kitty," Claire said softly. "My kitty."

Conrad gave her one last look as he turned to leave and then let out a mighty roar. Rusty barked a reply, and Darrell answered as well with a loud, "Thanks, boy!" He then hurried to Claire and covered her up. She still held on to her sippy cup.

Radioing the chief, Darrell waited for him to respond.

O'Hara asked, "You have her? Yes, is it good?"

"Listen for yourself. Say hello to the chief, Claire."

"Hello." O'Hara heard a child's voice come over the radio. "Mama, where are you?"

Now hollering as loudly as he possibly could, the chief yelled, "We got her, and she's okay! They're coming in!"

As the rescue team prepared to get Claire medical help as soon as she arrived, the father of the girl fell to his knees, saying through tears, "I can't believe it. Thank you, God, and thank all of you!"

***

Up in the cabin, Darlene napped restlessly. She was falling and then trying to get away and hide from someone. She awoke and realized it was only a bad dream. She got up, and after drinking some tea, she opened the back door. It was cold, but she felt no snow. Grabbing her coat, she headed down the path to the garden. As she found her bench, she sat down slowly. Someone watched her from the edge of the woods.

As Darrell and Rusty got Claire safely back to base camp, reporters hurried to capture the picture of the now-famous tracker, but he had something else on his mind.

"I have to go, Chief," he told his friend. "I have somewhere I got to be."

"Darrell, how can anyone ever thank you for what you've done for us?"

With a smile on his face, the tracker said, "I'd love to tell you sometime. C'mon, Rusty." And off they went.

***

Darlene's parents were almost to the cabin. They were excited to hear on the radio that the little girl had been found safe. "A miracle," Mr. Rivers had said.

The parents both wanted to be with their daughter in case things went bad. Darlene had been through tragedy before, and she was sensitive about things. Now as they made it up the driveway, they noticed Darrell's truck following them.

As they got out, they greeted him. Mr. Rivers said, "Nice job, old friend."

"We were lucky," Darrell exclaimed, "and that's why I'm here. I need to talk to you both and Darlene."

"What about?" Mrs. Rivers asked.

"Well, let's find your daughter, and I'll explain."

The parents then opened the front door, and they all went in.

"Darlene!" Mrs. Rivers looked in each room, but her daughter was nowhere to be found. "Oh, no!" she gasped.

"It's okay, dear. We'll find her," the father assured his wife, although a look of concern did come over his face.

Darrell headed to the back door. "Would she go outside?"

"Possibly," Mr. Rivers answered.

The three walked down the path toward the garden. Up ahead, they could see something near the bench.

"Darlene!" her mother called out. And then to her complete horror, she saw the mighty tiger as it lay next to her daughter.

The girl's arms were wrapped around his giant body, and her head rested against his.

"Oh, no, Darlene!" her mom called out.

The huge beast slowly stood up. Darrell quickly put his hand out in front of the girl's parents.

"Don't be scared, Mom," Darlene softly said. "It's Conrad, and he came back for me."

M. Savarese '18

Wilderness

Onward the tiger walked. It seemed a very long time before he felt safe to stop. Thirsty and hungry, he continued on his way. At a stream, he finally stopped to drink. A movement in the water caught his attention. Instinct told him to grab at this thing, and within minutes, he had it in his mouth.

Crunching down on this wriggling mass, the cat tasted blood, and then an unusual flavor followed. As hungry as he was, it tasted quite good. For now, he knew food was here if he needed it.

His hunting skills improved as time went by. With a variety of game to choose from, Conrad grew fast, strong, and carefree. Only one being could take him from his paradise, so from time to time, longing for her, he went back. Each visit he would watch and wait for the one thing he loved: Darlene.

Roaming in this new area, the tiger encountered many living creatures but didn't understand why he felt so out of place among all of them, yet something told him he was different. He had distant memories of his loving mother, and sometimes he dreamed of her and remembered. While slumbering fitfully, thoughts swirled through his head as he continued to dream.

One day as he was hunting for food, he ran smack into a large cat. Upon seeing the tiger, the other cat growled a very ferocious snarl. Not about to lose his hunting grounds, Conrad came up with an equally aggressive roar that startled the other cat and caused it to back off and head in the other direction.

Hmm, the tiger thought. *It worked.* He then watched satisfied as the mountain lion looked back several times and left the area. A few days later, Conrad headed toward his old stomping grounds. There was a chill in the air as he crept cautiously through the forest. But he couldn't help himself. He had to see her.

As he walked, his nose picked up two scents: one was very familiar and one was different, a human scent. He continued on when a distress sound made his ears prick up. He turned and headed in their direction.

As he started toward those sounds, the familiar scent entered his nostrils. Standing his ground, he watched as the mountain lion slowly came into view. Conrad thought there would be a showdown, but once again, the cougar thought better of it, did an about-face, and walked away.

The mighty tiger then continued on toward the sound of crying. Hours went by as Conrad guarded the tiny figure he had found. When Darrell and Rusty rounded the bend, he stood up. Upon seeing the figures, he realized the two were allies. He knew their scent and remembered how they had helped Darlene once. So as they came forward, he retreated to let them help the child. Looking back at them, he roared an acknowledgment that they both understood and then continued on.

***

"I got here as fast as I could," Darrell exclaimed, wondering what news the chief had to tell him. O'Hara stood with his finger on his chin as he told the tracker all about the other Sullivan brother that was in prison.

"Carl has a brother in prison," Darrell repeated.

"Yes," replied the chief. "An informant has told us that this guy's been running his mouth a lot. He blames the cops and the girl for his brother's death, and he's talking revenge."

"We need to inform the Rivers family right away. If this brother has connections, there is a lot he could possibly get done, even on the outside. I'll warn them to take precautions."

"Yes, good idea," agreed the chief. "By the way, there is a third brother. I did some background checks. The two older ones were always in trouble, but the younger one is a pretty decent guy, actually works in a veterinarian's office."

"Well, one out of three isn't that bad, huh?" Darrell grinned.

With a snide laugh, the chief shook his head.

The Reunion

Darlene stood up next to her beloved friend, knowing the time had come to explain how Conrad had entered her life. She sensed her mother's fear and spoke softly. As she began, the tiger eased back and lay down.

"Mom, Dad, Darrell," she began, "Conrad's been visiting me for a while, and although he is rather large now, he is gentle and kind. I know he would never hurt us. He saved me once and is quite protective of me, even now."

Conrad then opened his mouth and yawned.

Mrs. Rivers then exclaimed, "Where did he come from?"

"Mom, let's go inside out of the cold, and I'll explain everything."

As the foursome started to walk down the path together, Conrad slowly stood up and gently nudged Darlene. Reaching for the large head, she gently scratched his ears. She continued to coo, "I love you, Conrad," as she held him close. He responded with a strange but familiar purr. Then he turned around and walked quietly away.

"Darlene," Mrs. Rivers said softly to her daughter, "I can see you two have a special bond, and it seems he wants to keep you safe."

"Precisely," Darrell interrupted. "After all, Conrad is the reason we found the missing child. He found her on his way to visit Darlene."

"Well, then, intimidating as he is, he's good to have around in a pinch," Mr. Rivers added.

The next day, Mr. and Mrs. Rivers stood on the balcony and watched their daughter cradle the full-grown Siberian tiger's head in her lap.

Mrs. Rivers said. "It's unbelievable that all this time our daughter has been hiding this huge tiger from us and we didn't even know about him."

"Well, dear, maybe Darlene thought we would never understand the situation, and even after seeing them together, it is still quite a shock. She did tell me she was afraid if people knew of him, they'd come and take him away."

"Oh, Jim!" Darlene's mother cried out. "It is very scary, but she loves him so, it seems."

"Yes, dear, she certainly does, and you can see he loves her too."

"But he's so big," Mrs. Rivers went on.

"Yep, that he is," the father agreed. "That he is."

Darlene cooed to the massive head and spoke to her best friend. "Conrad, my sweet, sweet kitten, I've been told there might be danger in our future, so please, please try to be extra careful. I love you so much that if anything happened to you because of me, well, I would be heartbroken." She then bent down and kissed the cat gently on his head as he nudged her a little more roughly than usual, almost as if he needed to let her know that he wouldn't let anyone ever hurt her.

They were a team and not one to be trifled with. He then let out a loud roar to go along with it.

Darlene giggled softly back at him, saying, "You do understand me, don't you?"

As the young girl's parents watched from above, they couldn't believe the scene below.

"Is he talking to her?" Mrs. Rivers asked.

"Well, it sure sounds like it," the father replied.

As Darlene got up to walk the path home, Conrad watched her until she made it to the house. As she stopped at the door, she turned and yelled to him, "I love you, Conrad. Please come back soon."

He roared a mighty roar as he headed into the forest.

Two Heads Together

Gary sat at his desk and pondered the whole situation. His brothers' troubles had never been his, but lately it seemed that they had become so. With one brother dead and the other in prison, he felt this heavy weight on his shoulders alone. He had a pretty decent life with his job and all and enjoyed taking care of animals. So why was Steve pushing him all the time?

Then he remembered his mother's last words before she died. "You are brothers. Take care of each other."

Those thoughts swirled through his head as he drove to the prison to visit his brother.

M. Savarese '19

Silent Enemy

"Oh, Dad, are you serious?"

"Well, sweetie," Mr. Rivers tried to explain to his headstrong daughter. "It would make me feel a lot better. And yes, Darlene, I do know better than most. You may be blind, but you're certainly not helpless. You've proven that you can take care of yourself in many ways. It's just that your mom and I are getting older. It's just a little extra precaution."

Darlene turned toward her father. "Come hither." She giggled and held out her arms.

Her father immediately hugged his beloved daughter. His heart so overflowed with love for her that it pained him. When he was told at her birth that she was blind, it broke him down. As his little girl grew, he realized she developed like any other child. She flourished at her school and learned quite quickly. He had built the cabin and the lovely garden just for her. It had every special necessity he could come up with. It was her home now, and she loved it.

"Okay, Dad, how is it going to happen?"

"Well, honey, Darrell has a friend he knows from his army days who has special skills."

"Hmm," Darlene replied. "This might be interesting after all."

"Yes," her smiling dad added, "I thought that might get your attention."

Darrell drove up the winding road until he saw the tree with the camera. He knew where it was, so he waved. As he continued driving, he looked at his trusted friend, Rusty.

"Hey, boy, we're almost there."

An excited bark answered him. Finally reaching the gate, he watched as his old army buddy stood by to unlock it.

"Hey, Dan," Darrell called out.

As his friend greeted him, Darrell parked his truck, and they all walked up to the house.

"Okay," Dan said to the famous tracker. "Tell me all about this young woman and this friend she has visiting her every so often."

"She's a hell of a girl," Darrell began. "A hell of a girl."

After the meeting, they enjoyed the meal Dan had made. As the tracker and his dog prepared to leave, Dan stopped them.

"How big is this best friend she has?" He smirked.

"Put it this way. Let's be glad he's one of the good guys." The tracker grinned back as he drove away.

Darlene sat on the porch outside beside her mom, and together they listened to the sounds of the forest.

Mrs. Rivers noticed her daughter's somber mood. "Sweetie, what's wrong?"

"Well," Darlene answered, "I was thinking about what Dad said, how you both were getting older. I want you both here with me always."

"Oh my goodness," her mom exclaimed. "We're not going anywhere anytime soon, okay?"

Darlene reached out for her mother. "Okay, Mom; it's just I love you so."

"Us, too, dear, and besides you have a special friend whom I don't think will ever abandon you."

"Yes," Darlene agreed. "I do have him."

***

In the city of Lancaster at the state prison, two brothers, Steve and Gary, sat down to talk.

The convict, Steve, spoke first. "Well, are you doing it?"

"Yes, I've been trying my best, but the house is protected now. Cameras. Locked gate."

"She's blind, though, Gary. C'mon. You've got to somehow get past all that."

"I know, Steve. I will. I just need some more time. Those cops are going to pay for what they did to Carl."

"One way or another and since I'm stuck in here, it's all on you," Steve complained to his younger brother.

Gary's thoughts ran deep. "I know he was our brother, but why did he go there?"

"Don't give me that," Steve whispered. "They are going to pay. Mountain lion or not, they caused his death. Remember: our brother's gone. Don't forget that."

***

As Darrell drove Darlene to Dan's, they talked about the army buddies' friendship.

"Well," Darrell told her, "besides Rusty of course, he is

one person I'd trust my life to. He's good people, but as your dad might have told you, he's well trained in certain areas that might benefit you."

"We'll see soon," the amused girl replied.

As Dan greeted the two, he was very gentle as he took Darlene's hand. "I'm glad to meet you, miss."

"And I as well," she replied.

"I'll be back in a while, you two," Darrell said as he got back in his truck. "Be nice to each other," he added with a smile.

"Bye, Darrell," Darlene and Dan chorused.

As the two walked up to a building at the back of Dan's house, he spoke softly to Darlene. "Miss, I know this whole thing seems strange, but I promise you one thing. I won't teach you anything that makes you uncomfortable. You let me know, okay?"

"Yes, I will," the young woman answered.

"Okay, then. Let's first get to know each other," Dan said as he unlocked the door.

As the days went by, Darlene trained three times a week. It was the most difficult thing she had ever endured. There was one good thing coming out of all the hard work, though: she was learning.

***

"Okay, tell me what you saw," Steve said to his brother.

"I'll tell you," Gary answered, "but you aren't going to believe me. She was lying on the ground next to a huge tiger."

"What!" Steve gasped.

"You heard me right. She has a tiger."

36

The older brother put his fist to his chin. "There's only one explanation: those bastards left the cub. It's got to be him, and he killed Carl." Steve then leaned closer to his brother and whispered, "I want him." His voice got even lower. "I want him dead."

***

Darlene stood in the middle of a circle surrounded by swaying punching bags. Her teacher held one against his chest.

"You ready, Darlene?"

But before she could answer, a bag flew at her. She heard its sound like a snake feels vibrations, and fast as lightning, she counterattacked by punching it and moving out of the way. On and on the bags were shoved at her. She dodged them all.

"Very good, girl, but don't get overly confident. They'll have weapons, and they can see."

"Yes, sensei, I do know that. But it was pretty good, right?"

After lunch, Dan continued, "We'll practice our blocks and kicks."

With a half-smile, Darlene repeated, "But it was pretty good, right?"

"Yes, Darlene," he answered. "Yes, it was."

***

Conrad walked slowly in the forest. He listened to the sounds. Everything seemed as it should be. As he'd hunted the day before, there had been strange odors in the air. He avoided those smells when he could. With human smells, he seemed to understand the good ones from the bad. He knew her scent and realized as she spent most of her time in the cabin now, he must come closer to those odors. He had to. He knew she would always need him. He would stay closer.

***

Gary stayed hidden by the cabin. He watched the Rivers family closely. He saw Darlene's comings and goings. He watched as Darrell picked her up, and he kept the rifle aimed and ready and waited.

Darlene was excited about her parents' upcoming fortieth anniversary. She with the help of her aunt had planned a small get-together at the cabin. Just a few people, her mom had said.

Darlene had made a small list, and Dan and Darrell had happily RSVP'd.

"Wouldn't miss it." Darrell smiled. "I'll even bring a date."

"Good." Darlene giggled. "And if the date isn't Rusty, then he's more than welcome too."

The tracker had to admit it usually was the dog.

***

Gary prepared himself again for his trip. All his research and thoughts seemed to ransack his brain. Because he knew he didn't ask for all this trouble, the words of his mother drove him forward. Although he knew what had to be done, he couldn't stop the feelings he felt. Still family came first, and with that last thought, he put the guns in the bag.

Once in the car, he remembered his shock at the first sight of the tiger and that it had survived at all. "Unbelievable," he said under his breath.

***

The night of the party arrived, and as the cars made their way up the mountain, someone watched and wondered.

"Mom," Darlene asked her mother, "are you having fun?"

Mrs. Rivers took her daughter's hand in her own. "Sweetie," she gently answered, "I'm having the time of my life. This night is perfect, and I have everything I've ever wanted."

The young woman was just about to hug her mother when Rusty started barking excitedly.

"Wonder what that's all about," said Mrs. Rivers.

"It sounds like he's in the garden," Darlene replied. "Tell Dad to get his gun. I'll try to find out what's going on."

"Be careful, sweetie," her mom called out.

Gary watched as the dog ran up and down the path in the fenced enclosure. He knew the dog must know he was hiding in the thicket. He started to get up when the dog's demeanor changed.

It was starting to get dark, but as the stalker lifted his head, he saw him. He strode mightily toward the gate. He was a sight. Gary wavered in his vow to shoot, but after all, this beast had killed his brother.

As he took aim, his eye caught sight of Darrell as he grabbed for the gun. Quick as lightning, Gary grabbed his knife and struck the tracker in the leg. As Darrell fell back, he screamed out to Darlene.

Down the hill, Gary ran with his rifle aimed at the tiger

that turned as the shot came at him. With a roar, Conrad fell. Darlene heard that roar and made her way to the gate. Rusty followed her, barking loudly.

"No, boy. Stay," she told him as she unlocked the gate.

Knowing the beast was hit, Gary cautiously moved forward. The light near the enclosure shone brightly in the garden, and he could see Rusty jumping wildly while trying to get out. But where was the girl?

Then he saw her. She knelt by the massive figure on the ground. When Conrad saw Gary, he tried to rise, but he had been hit in the flank. He roared a warning to the intruder as the girl stood up.

Knowing she was blind, Carl's younger brother moved toward her. "I don't want to hurt you. I want the tiger. He killed my brother." His arm went up, and he aimed a gun once more.

Before he could shoot, Darlene's leg shot out and kicked the gun. It flew up in the air and fell several feet away. Gary ran at her. She heard the sound and blocked and punched him hard.

"Your brother was the killer!" she screamed.

As the man scrambled, he tripped and fell. Now the young woman remembered her training and brought a well-aimed kick down on the form. Gary lay motionless. Soon Darlene heard voices running down the path.

She called out, "Mom, Dad. Call Dan, please, and hurry. Conrad's been shot."

Darrell managed to make it to the house, and with a hasty warning, Chief O'Hara was on his way. Dan arrived and made his way to the garden. Several people called out to him.

"Darlene, I'm coming," he called to the girl.

He saw her father standing over Gary with a gun.

Darlene knelt on the ground. "Dan, he shot Conrad," she cried. "Is he dead?"

Dan went over and saw a large Siberian tiger lying next to her. As he touched the flank, he realized the cat was very much alive. He pulled a large dart from the fur. Conrad was only tranquilized. The intruder Gary must have known it was not wise to wound a tiger, so he chose a strong sedative to put him out first.

"Yes, he is alive, Darlene. Just asleep and he'll wake up in a while. Until then, we'll shelter him."

Chief O'Hara ran toward the group and stopped in his tracks. "Darrell warned me, but I simply can't believe what I'm seeing."

"Yes," Dan replied. "It's Conrad, and he came back for Darlene."

Epilogue

"A gift for my loving daughter," Mr. Rivers said as he handed Darlene the papers.

"Oh, Father, thank you," she gasped.

Her dad had purchased all the acreage he could around the mountain so Conrad would be safer. He could roam more freely in the new sanctuary. Darlene was completely happy. Everything in her life seemed perfect now. Dan and Darrell stopped by often, as did Chief O'Hara. Her parents had moved into the cabin with her, and life was wonderful. More often than ever, he strode into the garden. He made it all complete.

When he did show up, Darlene would coo to the large cat, "Conrad, my sweet, sweet kitten."

One Year Later

As the large truck drove around the winding road, its engine sputtered several times and then stopped. The driver tried to restart it, but to no avail. The couple then continued to argue about the cargo inside.

"What do we do now?" the girl yelled.

"We'll just let it go," said the man.

"What? Just leave it? We'll take the bike and leave the truck. No one knows about us," he continued. "We're just the drivers."

"Okay," they agreed.

The female finally reached into the truck and unlocked the cage inside. She looked into the cat's eyes and whispered, "I have to at least give you a chance. It's a big world out there. Take care of yourself."

As the motorcycle took off, a family drove past.

"Hmm," said the mother. "Looks like an abandoned truck."

As they moved on through the mountains, they continued to converse.

"Yes, he's learning quite fast," the young mother commented.

Their young son continued to turn the pages in his book when he excitedly called out, "Tiger! Tiger!"

The mother could see that the page showed a lion on it. She turned to the father, saying out loud, "Well, he never got that one wrong before."

The boy then leaned far around to look as the giant tiger disappeared into the forest.

Two Years Later

As the fire raged toward the small town and the residents evacuated, many told a tale of being woken up by loud roars and even seeing what looked to be two tigers moving quickly through the area, sounding off the warning that helped them escape.

Never the End

Although the story Conrad is a fictional account of a tiger that was kept in a backyard, the author hopes to help recognize this continues to be so.

She prays that laws help bring change in every state to stop these beautiful animals from being taken from their natural habitat and bred for profit. For every animal that improved a human's life, thank you.